D1392905

King Rat

DAINGEAN

2 8 JUN 2022

WITHDRAWN

Collins

R E D

STORYBOOK

Other Collins Red Storybooks to enjoy

King Rat

Bernard Ashley

Illustrated by Mark Robertson

Collins
An imprint of HarperCollinsPublishers

Leabharlann
Chontae Uibh Fhaill

Class JF

Acc 995/1186

Inv 995/14

£ 3·99 S/4

£4·60 R

First published in Great Britain by Collins in 1998
Collins is an imprint of HarperCollins*Publishers* Ltd
77-85 Fulham Palace Road, Hammersmith, London W6 8JB

1 3 5 7 9 8 6 4 2

Text copyright © Bernard Ashley 1998
Illustrations copyright © Mark Robertson 1998

ISBN 0 00 675338 8

The author and illustrator assert the moral right to
be identified as the author and illustrator of the work.

Printed and bound in Great Britain by
Caledonian International Book Manufacturing Ltd,
Glasgow G64

Conditions of Sale
This book is sold subject to the condition
that it shall not, by way of trade or otherwise,
be lent, re-sold, hired out or otherwise circulated
without the publisher's prior consent in any form,
binding or cover other than that in which it is
published and without a similar condition
including this condition being imposed
on the subsequent purchaser.

CONTENTS

CHAPTER ONE

Josh got out of the car and slammed the door just as if he'd paid his mum to drive him. With his nose held high where his eyes should be, he walked with her to the theatre, and wouldn't hold hands except for crossing roads. He had a swing to his walk which said he knew someone who was acting in the pantomime.

And he did. His sister Poppy was one of the Peggy Smith Sunbeams. She went to ballet and tap, and she was in the show this year, *Dick Whittington*. Today Josh was going to the dress rehearsal, when they were doing it for the first time with the lights and the music and the costumes.

Josh had never been to a theatre before. This theatre was called The Grand, old and gold and sneezy with dust. But it had a bar for drinks, and a place for buying light wands and cat masks and big red spotted hankies. He wouldn't have minded a wand or a cat mask, but he didn't want a hankie, thanks, he'd got a tissue. In the bar they met up with Dad, who'd brought Poppy early. There was just time for a Coke and a tiddle, before they sat in their seats in row A.

They hadn't been there long when the lights went out, very slowly. People stopped talking, and with a sudden roll on the drum and a whizz along the keyboard, up went the curtain. There was a rush of cold air and a smell of paint. And a great feeling of magic!

What Josh saw sat him back in his seat. It was so big, so bright, so loud. He looked this side and that, and tried to see it all at once. Sunny lights and a painted street – and there was Poppy

dancing and singing with the other Sunbeams. She looked so pretty that Josh wanted to smile his mouth up to his ears, and cry at the same time. His stomach went bubbly and his heart thumped as if he'd just *run* all the way to the theatre. He looked at his mum and he looked at his dad; Mum doing the same smiling as Josh, and Dad wiping his eyes.

Perhaps that was what those spotted hankies were for. This was like nothing he'd ever seen in his life.

When the first scene ended people clapped their hands and whistled, but no one clapped harder than Josh. He did it high in the air, for Poppy to see. Until Dick Whittington came on, carrying one of those same spotted hankies tied to the end of a stick – with his packed lunch in it. And with him came a cat as big as a person.

This was miles better than the telly, Josh reckoned. You could shout back at Dick, and at

Idle Jack – and Sarah the Cook threw sweets at you. Best of all, the cat jumped into the audience and patted a man's bald head; and when he went back, Dick said, 'Come home, Cat, come *hooom*,' in a silly way. It was like a party, only better.

Poppy came on a couple more times, but only running across and watching, until just before the end of the first half when she was in another big dance. With all the rest she waved goodbye to Dick and the cat, who were going off on a ship to Morocco to get rid of a plague of rats. But Josh saw only her. And all he heard were the proud noises Dad made in his throat.

In the interval they went back to the bar. But Josh couldn't wait for the second half. This was a brilliant treat.

CHAPTER TWO

The pantomime started again in Morocco. And there was Poppy, changed into a little slave girl and dressed as if she could catch cold. This time she wasn't just pretty, she was beautiful! When Josh clapped at the end of the dance, clapping wasn't enough. He stood up and shouted, the way he did at football.

When, *crash*! The stage went black. Lightning flashed. The music screamed. And Josh sat down, quick. In a great green volcano of smoke, up shot an enormous rat. He came like a rocket out of the floor – a *huge* rat, bigger than the cat, bigger than Dad, with a devil's face and a horrible get-you-in-the-night voice. And with a long grey tail which could come over and touch Josh if it was swished round hard.

Josh went stiff; shocked and scared. He tried to put himself through the back of his seat.

'*Mum!*'

He screamed, and shouted, and cried, and he couldn't stop. People were hissing and booing the rat, but the rat seemed to like it, it only made him worse. He did rat clawings at everyone, and bent over the front seats, closer, and closer. Now Josh strangled at his mum, and he shook, and he pulled her to get him out of that place and miles away from this horrible creature.

'Silly! It's only pretend!' she said.

But Josh's legs wouldn't stop twitching, and he couldn't open his eyes. His crying got to be hiccups as well.

'Come on.' She took him out to the bar. A First Aid woman tried to help, but all Josh

wanted was to sit on his mum's lap and hug her.

'What was it?' the First Aid woman asked.

'King Rat!' Josh's mother said.

'Yes, he's good, isn't he?'

'He's *horrible*!' Josh wailed.

CHAPTER THREE

There was no going back inside for Josh. Not even the promise of seeing Poppy again could get him through that door. He was like someone who'd just missed having a bad accident. He went on shaking even after he'd stopped crying. And he never wanted to come to a theatre again, ever. He hated Poppy for being in a show that made people cry and gave them the shaking hiccups. When he closed his eyes all he could see was that rat. And in his ears all he could hear was that tear-out-your-heart demon's voice.

Josh's mum looked at her watch. 'If my husband comes out, we're going for a walk,' she said to the First Aid woman.

'How will I know him?' she asked.

'He'll be the father of the little boy who cried!'

The little boy who cried! That's who Josh was. *The little boy who cried*. The baby. It was a rotten feeling, having a bad scare, because after you felt bad about feeling bad. It made your insides go worse than ever. It made your throat feel as if you'd swallowed a peach stone. It made your head hurt on the inside. It was like when Josh had had a big row, or got into bad trouble – it felt so twisted into him that it put a new mean look on his face.

Josh's mum got their coats from the cloakroom and took him out into the town. It seemed strange out there, still light, still people shopping. She held his hand – and he didn't mind it this time. Now his nose was where his chin usually was.

She walked him away from the shops and up one of the back streets, where people lived. It was in the direction that the car was parked, but they weren't going home yet. They had to wait for Poppy to finish. All the time Mum talked to him about how pantomimes were about people *pretending*. Davey Davis was off the television, he wasn't really Dick Whittington, was he? He was pretending. Poppy wasn't a slave girl, was she? She was pretending, too. They were all pretending.

'Well, I didn't pretend to get scared!' Josh said. 'That was real!'

CHAPTER FOUR

When they got back to the theatre, the pantomime was over. People were waiting in the bar for their children and their friends to come round from behind the stage. Josh wanted to wait outside in the street, but his mum said it was too cold. They found Josh's dad, who was smiling, all sorry.

'You were a silly old boy, weren't you?'

'You mean little baby,' Josh said, gruff in his throat.

'Poppy was good. She got a loud clap at the end.'

'Good for Poppy!' Josh really never wanted to see any pretending again.

Bit by bit the bar cleared. The Peggy Smith Sunbeams came through and found their families, Poppy carrying a make-up case like a showbiz star. Mum and Dad hurried over to tell her how she was the best thing in it.

'Did *you* like it?' Poppy asked Josh.

'Not bad,' he said. Then he had to confess. 'I didn't see the end.'

'Oh, were *you* the one?' she asked. And she laughed. 'King Rat said there was one!'

Which didn't please Josh. 'You can't help it when something makes you jump out of your skin!'

A kind-faced man came over and crouched down by Josh. 'Don't feel bad. We all get scared sometimes,' he said.

Josh looked at him.

'I got scared the other week, by a horse in a field. It galloped up to me, and I ran for the gate – while my dear wife patted it and gave it a sugar

lump. Did I feel silly?!'

Josh knew the feeling.

'Listen, if you've had a scare, can I treat you to a Coke? It's only fair.' The man said it so that Josh's dad could hear. Josh's dad smiled, and nodded OK.

'Thanks.'

The man went to the bar and bought a shandy for himself and a Coke for Josh. Nothing for Poppy or anyone else. His face was really wrinkly, like Josh's grandad, and his eyes were twinkly, the same. He had a soft voice, and a little chuckly laugh.

'Do you know who I am?' the man asked.

Josh looked round. He had to be one of the Sunbeams' grandads. 'No.'

'I'm King Rat.'

CHAPTER FIVE

They were in the dressing room by the time Josh had got over the surprise: Josh, and King Rat – who was really called Ken Cantwell – and Josh's dad.

'See, here's old King Rat.' Hanging on a wire hanger was a scruffy looking man-sized Babygrow. 'Feel this.' The tail was filled with crumpled up newspaper. 'Now, the face is in two parts.' From off a hook he took a wrinkled, rubbery, mask – like a balloon that has lost its puff. 'The rest is this.' The actor showed Josh a box of stage make-up, jumbo face paints, all muddled up – and not scary at all. None of it

was scary.

'Now come with me.'

Ken Cantwell led Josh and his dad down under the stage. Just behind where the musicians sat was a wooden platform. It was like a little lift, with a sort of tray to stand on.

'When I get the word, I stand on this. I wrap my tail round me so it won't get stuck. And right on cue, the stage manager pushes a button, and up we go!'

Ken Cantwell pushed a button – and up went the little tray. Above it, a trap door on the stage opened and the tray stopped.

'That's slow,' said Josh.

'But it looks fast because I jump, and the music bangs and crashes, and they puff out the green smoke. See – it's all pretend.'

Josh smiled. It was good, seeing how it was all done. He bet Poppy hadn't been down here and been told all this.

'Now, I'll tell you what. I want you to come back next week and see the show again. You'll know just how it all happens when you see it. You'll know that King Rat is only old Ken Cantwell, who at this moment is dying for another shandy. And you won't be scared of *me*, then, will you?'

Josh shook his head. He sure wouldn't! It was great to be in on all the pretending.

CHAPTER SIX

Josh couldn't wait for Monday to come. His mum and dad were going to Poppy's first night, and now he was going as well. He made up his mind not to spoil it for any other kids in the audience. He wouldn't tell *them* how King Rat was done, how nice the man was inside the rat costume, how he came up on a little tray. If they got scared, they got scared. It was a chance they'd have to take.

Their seats were in row C this time – but when Josh stood up he could still see the trap door where King Rat would come up. It was just in front of the curtain, and still very close.

Already, his insides were starting to go electric. He was going to see Poppy be the best person in it again, and he was going to see King Rat do his special things – the things *he* knew the secrets about. Josh felt like someone who was *in* the pantomime. Very special.

When the curtain went up this time, he knew straight away where to look for Poppy. And he knew when the sweets were going to be thrown out, and when he had to shout at Idle Jack, and when the cat was going to come and pat someone's head. It was great to be one jump ahead.

In the interval he looked at some of the other children and started to feel sorry for them. There were a couple of little girls in the front row. They were in for a big shock when King Rat came up. But he didn't frighten them in advance. It might spoil it for them to know how the pretending worked.

The second half started. But why did *his* heart have to start thumping hard as soon as the slave people danced? Why did *he* get that funny pain while he was clapping Poppy at the end of it?

He soon knew. Suddenly it all went black again. *Crash* went the drums. *Flash* went the lights! *Puff* came the green volcano! And up shot King Rat with that horrible voice. King Rat with those clawing claws. 'Ah, ha, ha, ha, *haaaa*!' Not Ken Cantwell, not any nice actor who liked a glass of shandy, but King Rat, the same King Rat who had scared Josh inside out before. And it wasn't as if he'd ridden up on any wooden tray, he'd come springing out of the flames at the centre of the earth.

'*Mum*!' Josh clutched at her again.

'Josh!'

Everyone was hissing and booing King Rat, just like before. The little girls in the front row were standing up and throwing sweets at him,

shouting back louder than anyone.

'You *know* it's pretend.'

'Out! Out! Take me out!'

'Josh!'

'OUT!' Josh stamped, started to hit at his mum.

'Am I ever going to see Poppy finish?' Mum took him to the foyer, to the First Aid woman.

'King Rat again?' she asked.

Josh's mum nodded.

'It's only pretend,' the woman said. 'Underneath, he's only—'

But Josh was hitting out at her now. He knew all that. It didn't stop him feeling as if he'd just got hurt in a romp.

'The magic of the theatre!' Mum said.

CHAPTER SEVEN

Josh's mum bought a Coke for Josh – which he drank so fast that his scarey hiccups went all fizzy – and an orange juice for herself.

The First Aid woman looked across at her, rolling her bandages, checking her little white bag. 'Did King Rat scare *you*?' she asked her.

'He made my heart jump – yes.'

'It wouldn't be much of a panto if he didn't scare you, would it? It's the whole point, I reckon. He's *supposed* to give you a jump! Except, some people just do a little jump inside, and one or two jump out of their skins…'

Josh stared at the First Aid woman. That was

like him – out of his skin!

The woman came over and crouched down. 'They make him *look* evil with all the tricks they know. They give you all the signs and signals – lights, music, smoke, costume. That's good panto. While in real life…' She shook her head.

Josh was over the hiccups, starting to listen to her now.

'…in real life, really nasty things often don't look evil at all.' She stood up again, pointing out into the street. 'A car coming along too fast, with the driver's mind somewhere else. Or a nice *looking* stranger trying to give out sweets…'

Josh didn't nod, but he wanted to. He'd once had a real scare with a car where he could have got hurt. He knew what the woman meant. And he also knew that King Rat couldn't actually hurt him.

'At least old King Rat lets you know what he's about!' the First Aid woman said.

Josh's mum had been listening – and not listening. She had her face in two directions, now for the First Aid woman, now for the man who sold the drinks and the panto presents.

'And did you notice this?' she asked, coming back from the counter. She was holding up one of the big red spotted hankies, the sort Dick Whittington had carried for his packed lunch.

Josh looked at it. A spotted hankie? What about it?

'Did you notice how Dick always has his special hankie with him – even after he's come to London, and when he's in Morocco? It's round his neck, or on his head. He's always got it somewhere…'

'So?'

'It's what Nanna used to call 'a bravery flag'. Something he's always got, to make him feel right. Like you used to have your bit of blanket, and Poppy's got Old Ted…'

It was true. Dick did wear the hankie in every scene, now that Josh thought about it.

'Here, I've got *you* one. Now you can be like Dick Whittington. It makes him feel right, see if it does the same for you.' Josh's mum showed him his red spotted panto present. But somehow, by now, he wasn't feeling so bad. Not so bad at all…

CHAPTER EIGHT

There was a sudden big laugh and a cheer from inside the theatre. And it went on and on. Something was happening which had got everyone going. But Josh couldn't think what it was – because he'd never seen the panto this far.

'They're going for old King Rat,' the First Aid woman said. 'Giving him what for! You ought to see him, being chased by Cat and all the Sunbeams, getting his tail cut off!'

It sounded like good fun. Was Poppy doing the chasing? A scream of laughter went up.

'Funny, too!'

Josh wanted to find out. He slipped off his

chair and went to stand by the swing door into the theatre, putting an eye to the crack. Up on the stage, the cat was holding up King Rat's tail, while all the Sunbeam children were chasing him this side and that. And it *was* funny! All the kids in the audience were on their feet, shouting and pointing and laughing. King Rat slipped, King Rat tripped, King Rat bumped into the scenery. He dived through a window and came out covered in a line of knicker washing. Josh thought people's bellies would burst with laughing.

He slid through the door and stood at the back to see it better – just as King Rat jumped off the stage and started running backwards and forwards across the front, waving his hands in fear. Poppy was up on the stage, doing a dance with all the others to show they'd won. But Cat was still chasing – and King Rat was trapped at the front. The drummer stood up and bonked

him on the head with a tambourine. King Rat looked this way and that, and shouted 'Help!' and 'Mercy!' and suddenly came running up the centre aisle towards the back of the theatre.

Towards where Josh stood, with his mum behind him.

Josh's heart went pump. His eyes went big. His mouth dropped open. But he felt the spotted hankie being pushed into his hand.

King Rat ran nearer and nearer, still shouting for mercy and going 'Oooer!' – with the cat close behind, each in his own spotlight.

Right up to where Josh stood.

Up on the stage the scene changed, ready for the wedding of Dick and Alice. And here at the back the spotlight went out. King Rat's bit was over.

Cat slid past Josh in a hurry, to get back to the stage. But King Rat stood there with his hands on his hips, getting his breath back with a wheeze.

And he looked at Josh through the slits of his mask.

He crouched down low. 'It's Josh, isn't it?' he asked, in his kind Ken Cantwell voice.

Josh nodded.

'Well, come on, then, I've just got time. Are you going to buy me a shandy?'

Josh stared at him. And shook his head. 'No way!' he said – and stood back to give him a good hiss and a boo, waving his spotted hankie at him.

Until someone sitting near the back turned round and told him to shush.

Keep Out, Father Christmas!

CHAPTER ONE

Dick Whittington wasn't the only one on the move. Josh and Poppy were leaving their old home behind – although not to make their fortunes. Dick had set off for London where the streets were paved with gold, while the children were off to the edge of town, where the road was lined with trees. They were leaving their small rented house on the estate and going to a big old house which would be their own. But the move wasn't going to be easy.

'What a time of year to uproot yourself!' Mum said. 'Christmas!'

'It's a stupid time,' said Josh, beating Poppy to

the Advent calendar and opening the next window. 'How's Father Christmas going to know where we are? We sent him our letters from this place.' Then he got one up on Nosy the cat, in a race to the front door, as the postman put today's cards through.

Poppy left her pathetic little brother to be first at everything, and folded her arms to think about the problem. They hadn't sent letters up the chimney to Father Christmas because they didn't have fireplaces in this house. Instead, they'd posted them to him in the Co-op store in town. All the same, they'd got this *old* address on.

'Oh, you needn't worry about Santa finding you,' Mum said. 'He'll know where you are. He's good at all that.'

''Course he is,' Poppy joined in. 'Someone who gets all round the world in one night is magic enough to know about a change of address.'

Thinking about it, it made sense, didn't it?

'I'm still gonna send him one of our change of address cards, to make sure.'

'Do what you like.' And the look on Poppy's face was so *big sister* she nearly had it wiped off with a *little brother* swipe.

CHAPTER TWO

They had finished up at school till January – they'd had their parties and been given presents by the pretend Father Christmas, the school caretaker with a tattoo which the real Father Christmas wouldn't have. But them being on holiday didn't please their mother one bit – not with all the clearing and packing she had to do.

Because, just to make life difficult, *when* were they moving? Only two days before Christmas Eve, to get in before the moving people and the estate agents shut down for the break. How unhelpful could you get? *And* no time to get a change of address card to Father Christmas.

Mum and Dad wanted to move sooner, but they weren't allowed to – paperwork, or something – although they had been given a key to the new house, which was empty. That way they could measure up for curtains and think about how to cut their carpets.

Poppy was one bubble of excitement on the Saturday when she was first going to see the new place. She'd got a panto matinee at two o'clock – she liked doing the matinees, there were more children there to shout and boo at old King Rat – but the real buzz was the new house and her new bedroom. She'd only ever known their old house, and it was great to imagine living in the new one. Bigger rooms, an extra bit in the kitchen for a sit-up counter, and much more garden. And instead of deciding which things to have out because her bedroom was so small, in the new house there'd be room for her to have everything she wanted around her, all the time.

They captured Nosy, put her in the cat basket, and drove to the edge of town. They wanted Nosy to get the smell and the feel of the place, so she wouldn't go off on her usual nosing around when they moved. But the most important getting-used to was going to be for Poppy and Josh.

The car just about squeezed in to a little driveway at the front of the house. But if the front was titchy, the back garden was long and grassy, and bush and tree-y. And the house was big, the rooms were high, and the stairs were like the sort you see in a seaside hotel.

'Go up and look at your new rooms,' Mum said, 'we'll be down here measuring for blinds.'

Up the wide bare stairs went Josh and Poppy – up to where there was a bathroom and a separate lavatory, a big front bedroom for Mum and Dad, a middle-sized bedroom (still enormous) for Poppy, and Josh's smaller room at the back.

Straight off, Josh christened the lavatory, while Poppy went into the middle bedroom. Big and empty with bare boards, it was a space like the stage of The Grand, so there was nothing for it but to do the London town dance from *Dick Whittington* Act One.

'*That's why we love Lon-don Town...*' she sang, and posed in a finishing position – not even answering back when Josh passed her door and said, 'Show-off!'

Because she hadn't done her pantomine pose. Poppy's rigid pose was because she had suddenly frozen.

CHAPTER THREE

She was looking at the fireplace. It was a big fireplace, with a marble surround and a line of painted Victorian flower tiles down each side. And there was a big grate, where the last people would have had a real coal fire, with a sooty chimney going up.

Poppy came out of her freeze, backed away from the fireplace and went out of the door and along the landing to look at Josh's room.

It was smaller, without a fireplace but with a radiator instead, the sort they'd got in the other house, but nicer. The room was just wide enough for a window, which looked out over the garden,

and long enough for a single bed and a small wardrobe – about the size of Poppy's room back on the estate.

As she stood looking round, Josh was going on about whether he'd have his bed sideways across the window, or down the side, behind the door.

Poppy went over to see the view of the bushes and trees from up here, and, very quiet for her, she turned and went back downstairs to where the kitchen was being planned.

'Mum, Dad…'

They carried on with measures, pencils, and pads.

'*Mum…*'

A grunt

'*Dad…*'

'What is it? We're listening.'

But now there was nothing from Poppy.

'What is it?' Dad had accidentally dropped his

tape measure and was going to have to do the kitchen width again.

'I...'

Another nothing.

'I ...'

'You *what*?'

Now both of them were staring at her. Even Nosy, given the run of the kitchen while the front and back doors were shut, had stopped chasing the tape measure to look up at Poppy.

'You know the bedrooms...'

'Yes, we know the bedrooms. Where people sleep. In beds.'

More nothing, until just before their patience ran out altogether, 'Well, I want the little one.'

Dad cricked his neck looking round. 'The what?'

'The little one, the one at the back...'

'Josh's bedroom?'

'No, *my* bedroom. Josh can have the other one.'

Mum didn't understand, either. 'Poppy, you're bigger, you have the bigger room. It's your... your... it's what the bigger child has.'

'Unless the *bigger* one wants the *smaller* one,' Poppy argued. 'Then the *smaller* one can have the *bigger* one. It's the *bigger* one having the *bigger* choice, and the *smaller* one having the *smaller* choice. Only this *smaller* choice will be the *bigger* choice.'

Dad dropped the end of his tape measure again giving Nosy something to chase.

'Listen, girl, you've got a desk, a keyboard, a dolls-house that you can't play with because it's in the loft. You've got games galore and enough books for a library. You won't throw anything out – look at Old Ted. You want a computer for your birthday, and don't all teenage girls want stereos and all that?'

'She's not a teenage girl!' Mum threw in quickly.

'No, but she will be one day. Not to mention her wardrobe already big enough to stock Next.' He frowned at Poppy. 'Why go from small to small when you can go from small to big? I don't get it.'

Nosy miaowed – she'd lost the end of the tape. She didn't get it either.

'Because I like the view of the garden,' Poppy said. 'It's better from Josh's room – I mean, the back one. You can see all the trees right to the bottom. I can always fit in what I want.'

And she included Old Ted in that, whatever her dad said. Especially Old Ted. Old Ted was her teddy bear from years back, who'd once been a silvery grey, but now had no fur left except round behind his ears. He was smooth and thin, and where there had once been a belly button that squeaked, there was just a hard little disc that did nothing. But Poppy wasn't going to let anyone throw him out. She wanted him there when she needed him, Old Ted.

'I'll have the big room all right!' said Josh, who was leaning on the doorpost, hearing all this; and he raced back upstairs to check on his new space.

Poppy was near to tears. 'I just *want* it!'

'All right, don't cry, you've got a matinee,' said Mum.

'We'll sort it,' said Dad. 'We've got a week yet. Nothing's written in stone.'

Poppy didn't understand that. But she understood Josh, all right, when he came skidding back to stand looking all *top of the tree* in the doorway.

'I know why she doesn't want the room,' he told them.

Everyone's eyes were fixed on him, even Nosy's.

'She's scared,' he said. 'She's got the shivers.'

CHAPTER FOUR

After all Josh's shivers at King Rat, he nearly got into big trouble for that – especially since what he'd said *did* make Poppy cry, and with her matinee to do, too.

Dad made it clear that none of the rooms in this house was *haunted* or anything; and new big spaces did feel *different* to cosy little ones. But for the sake of the show the whole thing was quickly skated over, and 'left open' as Mum put it. They could make up their minds about bedrooms right at the last moment, even as the furniture came in from the van.

On the Monday, she took them into town to

choose some ready-made blinds from Do-It-All. For Poppy, it was a drag, but the promise of a McDonalds got her going.

Still wiping ice cream from their mouths, they walked back to the car past the Co-op, when Josh suddenly pulled out of his pocket his reason for coming shopping without a fuss. It was one of the change of address cards from the hall table. He'd filled it in for Father Christmas.

'I'm gonna make sure he knows,' he said.

Poppy snatched it for a look.

'With only *your* name on it?' she asked. 'How selfish can you get?'

'Tons more, if I want! Anyhow, you said as he's magic, he'd know, so what are you worried about?'

'You could have put me on, to make sure.'

'Well, I never did, so there!'

Mum gave both their arms a jerk. 'Don't you show me up in the street! Get inside, and get it posted.' She pulled Josh into the store, leaving Poppy to follow.

They went up to the first floor where the Christmas post box had been, but found themselves at the end of a queue of pushchairs, toddlers, infants and juniors waiting to get on the next Christmas train to the North Pole.

'Where's the post box?' Mum asked an assistant in a short Santa Girl skirt – which wouldn't suit the polar regions at all.

'All packed up, love, he's here in person instead.'

Josh went rigid. Poppy, too.

'*Who* is?' Mum asked.

'Father Christmas.'

'Where?'

'At the North Pole, the end of the train ride.' Santa's assistant smiled and turned to the children. 'And you can have your picture taken with him as a souvenir.'

'No, we're not into that expense,' Mum said. 'This one just wanted to let him know our new address, that's all.'

'Ah…' The assistant looked at the card Josh was holding. 'I'll take you round the back – see if we can slip it to him on the quiet.' She winked at them.

She led the way back past the toys for sale, behind the scenery of the train ride – like taking them round the back at a fairground.

Josh followed.

But Poppy found herself stuck where she was. She was going to wait here, thank you very much.

CHAPTER FIVE

Poppy reckoned she knew as much about Father Christmas as anyone. At school they'd heard about different Christmas traditions from all the different countries. Poppy knew how he was Saint Nicholas, or Father Noël, or Knecht Ruprecht. She knew how in some countries he was a bit strict, in others he wore different clothes. But the *real* Father Christmas, the *true* one, was the one she believed in: the merry, twinkly-eyed old man who was kind, and fond of a mince pie and a drop of Scotch. Someone who was magic enough to make all the presents for everyone, or buy in the ones with printed names. And she *did* believe in magic. There was a magician in the pantomime, and his magic was real, all right.

And her Father Christmas always had a long silvery-white beard. Which, if she were honest, was the reason she was a bit scared of him. He always looked at you with twinkly eyes from a face which seemed a bit like a mask. And his voice was usually low and *ho-ho-ho-ey*, more like the sort of voice her dad put on in a game of chase...

Poppy knew she was being stupid, but she just didn't want to go round the back of the train. All right, she told herself, a lot of people *dressed up* as Father Christmas – like the caretaker at school and Uncle Bill at parties – but you knew they were themselves underneath. These Father Christmases in the shops were the real Father Christmas's assistants – there were so many of them about they couldn't *all* be him – but they

came from the real one. They probably even went back to have tea with the real one, they were close to him. And she just didn't want to meet this one today. She'd leave it to Josh to make double sure he knew about their change of address.

Which he did. In no time, hardly missing Poppy at all, Josh and their mum came back and said that the Father Christmas had taken the card, and he'd thanked them. And Poppy's name had definitely been put on as well.

So there'd be no doubt at all that Father Christmas would be there to bring their presents to the new house.

CHAPTER SIX

That night they went round to the new house to put up the blinds in the kitchen. Straight off, Josh rushed upstairs to have a better look at his new bedroom – the big one in the middle – while Poppy tried to get herself used to being in the same sized bedroom as the one she'd got already. She had that upset feeling that comes when you've disappointed yourself – like saying she wouldn't do the duet with Dick Whittington in Act Two, and then being jealous of Mary Foster, who did.

She was looking out of the window at the garden, telling herself what a brilliant view it was, when Josh came thumping down the half landing and stood in her doorway.

'What do *you* want?'

'To tell you I know for sure, that's all.' He pulled a face at her and started to go.

'You know *what*, cleversticks?'

'I know why you don't like that other room.'

Poppy turned her head and looked out at her view again. 'I've told you why I don't like it. I like this view more than that one.'

'No way – you prefer this radiator.' He clanged it with his foot.

'*What*? Huh!'

'You want *no fireplace*, that's what you want.'

Poppy could feel herself going red, and the more she felt it, the more she couldn't stop it happening. 'Talk sense, boy!' she said, or croaked more like. 'Why wouldn't I like a stupid fireplace? You do talk a load of old—'

'Because of Father Christmas.'

'What?' She leant back on the window sill.

'You don't want him coming down the chimney into your bedroom. You're *scared* of Father Christmas.'

Poppy tried to hit him – but already Josh was legging it back to his room with the fireplace. She stopped. The beast! He knew, the little tyke. He knew what she didn't even want to admit to herself. He knew she was happy with the way things had been in the other house, where Father Christmas left all the presents downstairs, on the front mat, because they didn't have any chimneys.

And she wanted to cry – *because* Josh knew; and because it was the truth. She didn't fancy that magic old man with the long silvery-white beard coming into her bedroom, no matter what he brought. She just didn't.

CHAPTER SEVEN

'I'll board it up.'

Mum and Dad had got to hear about all this – how couldn't they in an empty house? And Dad had the answer straight off.

'I'll put a plywood front on the fireplace and paint it in to match the woodwork. I'll disguise it—'

'I'm not worried…' Poppy was still trying to hold her head up high.

'He'll know, Father Christmas. He knows when there's no exit – and he'll leave both your presents on the hearthrug in front of the big fireplace downstairs. Won't he, Mum?'

Mum nodded.

'Will he?' asked Josh. Because he'd wondered where the person without a fireplace in their room would leave the mince pies and Scotch before they went to bed. But his voice sounded a bit hollow – because with showing off to Poppy, he'd just done himself out of the bigger bedroom.

'It'll be my next job,' said Dad, 'now we've got the kitchen blinds up.' He smiled at Poppy. 'You're not unusual,' he said.

'She is, she's a monster from Mars.' Josh *was* cross with himself now.

Dad ignored him – he knew how Josh felt, as well. 'I was the same, Pops. Lots of people are. I don't like Mum in the kitchen when I'm cooking. She doesn't like me crowding her when she's using the phone. We all like our own space. Birds sing to warn other birds not to trespass. Goats soon have you out of their fields! So don't you feel bad about not wanting anyone in your

bedroom who doesn't knock at the door and ask to come in. Not even Father Christmas.'

'I don't mind, really,' said Poppy, feeling her eyes prickling for a cry.

'So I *won't* board in the fireplace, then?'

'No, do it,' she said. 'If you like. And I *will* have that room, if it's OK with Idle Jack.' She looked at Josh, who was prevented from making the face of all faces by Dad's next promise.

'And Josh can have the loft space when I've converted it.'

Now Poppy smiled. Suddenly, she was looking forward to the move again.

CHAPTER EIGHT

It's always easier moving from a small house to a bigger one – there isn't all the throwing out at one end and the fitting in to do at the other. And whether it was nearly Christmas Eve or not the move happened, with everybody's stuff ending up safely at the new address where it was put into this room, or that room, or the big front room called *Pending*.

As soon as they arrived, Poppy ran up the stairs ahead of the removal men with her first crate. She raced into her bedroom to check that the fireplace was boarded up. If not, she was having the smaller room...

And, *was it*? She had to look twice, she missed it the first time. Because what was there didn't look like a fireplace at all, it was more like the inside of a little theatre, when you're facing the stage. It was so clever she wanted to give it a clap. Clever, and just *right*, when she thought about it; after all, an old-fashioned fireplace looks like an old-fashioned theatre. The mantelpiece and the sides are just like the picture frame of the stage. So what Dad had done, on the boarded up bit in between, was paint front curtains, which looked just like those heavy red velvet tabs at The Grand.

Great! Everything was great, right down to Old Ted coming in sprawled on top of the crate as if he'd lived here all his life.

She wasn't even upset by the news that Nosy had disappeared. Well, Nosy was a wanderer.

'She'll be all right,' Mum said. 'She's around somewhere. Or we'll check back at the old house. She'll show up.'

So Poppy shut her bedroom door and started sorting her things. It was great having all this space – and room for more, when Father Christmas had brought her new presents.

CHAPTER NINE

By Christmas Eve they were more or less straight – except that Nosy was still on the missing list – and Christmas started to warm up for Mum and Dad, too.

'Christmas starts here!' Mum said, as she poured a sherry and put a tray of mince pies in the microwave.

The four of them went into the big front room, where there was an even bigger fireplace than Poppy's, and a special new rug on the floor across the front of it.

'This is where he'll leave your presents,' Dad told them, 'so we'll put his mince pies and something to drink on the mantelpiece.'

Poppy tingled at the thought of it all happening so soon now. Already, it was pyjamas and dressing-gowns for her and Josh; and, with Father Christmas's snacks in place, the word 'bed' came into the conversation.

'Try to get to sleep quickly,' Mum said – which Poppy reckoned was one of the daftest things anyone ever came out with. Thinking try-to-get-to-sleep thoughts only kept you awake, didn't they?

But they went up and Josh closed his door, and Poppy almost closed hers. With a last look round her new bedroom, she got into her new, bigger bed and cuddled the threadbare Old Ted. For a while she lay there listening to the sounds of a few friends coming in downstairs for Christmas Eve drinks, but she must have drifted off, because the next thing she knew, her door was shut, and her night-time plug in the electric socket was glowing. Someone had been up to snuggle her down.

It was Christmas Eve, dark and late. With another tingle, and another cuddle of Old Ted, Poppy realised that Father Christmas had to be about by now, somewhere in the world.

She turned her head into her pillow, excited, excited... Was he going to bring her any of the things she wanted? If so, which of them would they be? Her mind roamed over her list of wants.

But she'd only got to Barbie's Barbecue when – *what was that*? Suddenly, she was sitting up again. Had she heard a noise? Yes, it was definitely there – a noise she hadn't heard before in this room.

Something between a tapping and a knocking – and was that a soft voice she could hear?

Her mouth had gone as dry as old bread. The noise she could hear was coming from *behind* the

painted theatre curtains on her fireplace. *Tap-tap, knock-knock, sigh-sigh*. There was something behind there. Or there was someone!

And she only needed one guess as to who it was.

Chapter Ten

It must be Father Christmas – stuck! He'd got the message about the change of address, but he hadn't been told that the fireplace in Poppy's bedroom had been boarded up! His magic systems had blipped.

Poppy was out of bed and onto the landing like a flash of magic herself. She ran across to her parents' room and, without bothering to knock, swung straight in.

But the bed was empty. They were still downstairs.

She ran to the top of the stairs, to go down and fetch her dad, to get him to go in on his own to take off the plywood. She didn't want Father Christmas stuck, or going away without leaving her any presents.

But as Poppy looked over the banisters, she could see the door of the front room half open, and the Christmas guests still there; being fairly quiet because the children were in bed. And she saw her mother pouring and serving, telling them that Roger had gone to fetch Gran. Roger being Poppy's dad. *He wasn't there.*

Poppy panicked. By the time she got down to her busy mum and pulled her out of the party, wouldn't Father Christmas have given up?

She ran back to her room. There was nothing for it – there was no other way, unless Christmas was going to be cancelled for her. She'd have to ease off the boarding-up herself, make a little gap so that Father Christmas could push his way through while she ran and hid in Mum and Dad's room.

She switched on her light and listened, trying to hear things outside the gasping of her own breathing. She grabbed Old Ted off her bed and, step by step, she crept back to the fireplace.

Scuff. *Tap*. A muffled knock – and then a sound she didn't recognise, very quiet and throaty. Was he speaking in *North Polish*?

Now she was leaning towards the fireplace, no more than three-ply thickness away from Father Christmas himself. And, almost without thinking about it any more – just a look round to make sure the bedroom door was open – she got a finger behind an edge of the plywood, then two fingers, then three, and finally Old Ted's paw and her own hand. And together they pulled, to give Father Christmas the idea of where to push.

Miaow!

Father Christmas?!

More like Mother Cat! More like Nosy, mewing at the light and getting so excited she was turning round and round and sweeping soot off the back of the grate. The missing cat who'd got stuck up a tree and found her way back along the roofs – only to find a chimney which went down but not back up.

'*Nosy*!' Poppy pulled the cat through, and sat on the boards stroking her – fur, soot, and all.

'You're home, Cat, you're *hoooo*m!' she said – like Dick Whittington in the panto.

She looked at the bent and wobbly curtains on the front of her own Grand Theatre. And suddenly, while the cat jumped and ran off downstairs, she started tugging away at the rest of the boarding-up.

CHAPTER ELEVEN

She wasn't sure why she'd done that. Even when the guests had gone, and Nosy had been cleaned, and Poppy had had a good wash and a change of pyjamas – even after all that, she wasn't sure *why*.

She knew *what* she'd done. She'd opened up the fireplace for Father Christmas, that was what. But *why*, she definitely wasn't so sure about.

Was it because she'd suddenly found she hadn't been too scared to go close and pull at the plywood? Was it because she wanted Father Christmas to leave her some presents? Was it because having Old Ted in her other hand made her feel strong, made her a bit braver – like Josh with King Rat when he'd got his red spotted handkerchief?

Or was it because she *cared* about Father Christmas, so she hadn't been scared when she thought he was stuck, or hurt. So *not scared* that she didn't mind him coming in here, any more than she minded her mum and her dad? And was being scared and not scared like a pair of scales? Did it all depend what was in the other pan, to balance things?

She wasn't sure. What she *was* sure about was that next morning there'd be some presents for her up here in her room. She'd made sure of that, by putting the mince pies and Scotch on her own grate.

And after thinking it round and round it all became a dream as she finally fell asleep; Old Ted with his eyes always open by her side.

On the fireplace side of the bed…

Order Form

To order direct from the publishers, just make a list of the titles you want and fill in the form below:

Name ....

Address ....

....

....

Send to: Dept 6, HarperCollins Publishers Ltd, Westerhill Road, Bishopbriggs, Glasgow G64 2QT.

Please enclose a cheque or postal order to the value of the cover price, plus:

UK & BFPO: Add £1.00 for the first book, and 25p per copy for each additional book ordered.

Overseas and Eire: Add £2.95 service charge. Books will be sent by surface mail but quotes for airmail despatch will be given on request.

A 24-hour telephone ordering service is available to holders of Visa, MasterCard, Amex or Switch cards on 0141- 772 2281.

Collins
An *Imprint of* HarperCollins*Publishers*